Cinders
and
Sparks

MAGIC AT MIDNIGHT

Cinders and Sparks

MAGIC AT MIDNIGHT

LINDSEY KELK

Illustrated by Pippa Curnick

HARPER

An Imprint of HarperCollinsPublishers

Library of Congress Control Number: 2020951737
ISBN 978-0-06-300669-0
Typography by Corina Lupp
21 22 23 24 25   PC/BRR   10 9 8 7 6 5 4 3 2 1
❖
First published in Great Britain in 2019 by HarperCollins
Children's Books, a division of HarperCollins Publishers Ltd.
First US Edition, 2021

For Karrahan, Edie, and Ayse,

who are already magic

Chapter One

"**A** LONG TIME AGO, IN a kingdom far, far away, there lived a girl. And, even though the girl was humble and poor, she was as kind as she was beautiful and, whenever she passed by, all the townsfolk would say she was—"

"Incredibly boring?"

A young girl with messy hair and bright eyes stood in the doorway, yawning so hard her head almost fell right off her shoulders.

"Good morning, Cinders." Margery, the storyteller and the girl's stepmother, gave her a stern look. "Have you finished all your chores already?"

"Yes," said Cinders.

"You've chopped the wood?"

"Yes," said Cinders.

"You've fed the pigs?"

"Yes," said Cinders.

"Done all the dishes?"

Cinders looked back at the pile of plates, bowls, and saucepans stacked up in the sink. She had not done all the dishes. She had not done *any* of the dishes.

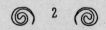

"Yes," said Cinders, swiftly stepping to the side to block her step-mother's view of the kitchen. "May I go outside now?"

"No," replied Margery, turning back to her book. "Ladies don't play outside."

"Ladies stay inside and sit nicely," Cinders's stepsister Agnes announced from her seat on the sofa. "Like us, listening to Mother reading. Ladies don't ruin their dresses in the mud as you always do."

"I like reading, but I like reading for myself, not listening to Margery," Cinders muttered, scratching at a stain on the hem of her dress. What had she spilled on it that was purple? "She doesn't do all the voices. And I'd rather read outside, not cooped up in here. Sometimes it gets a bit muddy—I can't help that."

"I wouldn't mind reading outside," piped up Eleanor. "It's a lovely day. Maybe I'd like it."

"You wouldn't like it at all," Agnes informed her little sister. "There are bugs everywhere, and it would be no good at all for your complexion. You want to stay inside with me and Mother."

"Do I?" Eleanor replied with a shrug. "If you say so . . ."

"As I was saying before I was so rudely interrupted," Margery said, turning her back to Cinders, "there was a beautiful girl in a faraway kingdom and she was loved by everyone she met. She was good and truthful, and she never lied to her stepmother about finishing her chores when there was clearly a sink full of dishes waiting to be washed."

Cinders sloped back into the kitchen, turned on the tap, and stared out the window.

Not for the first time she wished the elves would make some kind of device for washing dishes instead of just useless things like phones for playing games. A washy-dishy-thingy. Hmm. The name might need work.

Cinders sighed. Trust Eleanor to side with Agnes. They always ganged up against her. Before her father had remarried, she'd dreamed of having a loving mother and a sibling to play with, but instead she'd been saddled with Miserable Margery and the Terrible Twosome. Margery wasn't *so* bad, but she thought about nothing but herself and how she looked and what people thought of her and her girls. She was always nagging Cinders, punishing her messiness and forgetfulness with chores, chores, and more chores. It hadn't been so bad when they'd first come to live in her pink cottage at the edge of the woods, but as they'd gotten older, Cinders had realized her stepmother was always going to be bossy and boring, and that she and her stepsisters had absolutely nothing in common.

When she was inside, Cinders was always covered in glitter and glue or had paint in her hair. When she was outside, she loved to climb trees and chase her dog, Sparks, around the forest. Elly and Aggy hated to leave the house unless they were absolutely forced to do so. Their idea of a dreamy afternoon was poring over pictures of Prince Joderick before discussing the very latest trends in ribbon tying, or taking photos of themselves. More than anything, they hated the idea of any activity that might get them dirty. Cinders couldn't remember the last time she wasn't head to toe in mud by the end of the day. All she wanted was an adventure. All her stepsisters wanted was a new elf phone.

Staring at the stack of dirty dishes, she sighed. "I'm going to be stuck here forever," she muttered under her breath, fixing her big green eyes on the bright blue sky above.

"I wish these dishes would wash themselves."

Cinders reached out for a dirty plate, but before she could even

touch it she felt a jolt shoot through her hands. The plate jumped off its pile, plopped into the sink, and disappeared under the bubbles with a splash.

Margery, Elly, and Aggy all looked up at once at the sound.

"Nothing to see here," Cinders called to them, smiling like a loon. "Just me, washing the dishes—same old, same old."

Fishing around in the sink, she hunted for the

missing piece of china in a panic. If she broke another plate, she'd be scrubbing the toilet for a month. Suddenly the plate flew up out of the sink and set itself on the kitchen table, squeaky clean and bone dry.

"But I didn't even touch you," Cinders whispered, pulling her hands out of the water. "What is happening?"

One by one, all the dirty dishes whizzed themselves into the sink and out again, piling up neatly on the table.

Cinders gazed at her fizzing fingertips, holding them up in the sunlight. Were they *sparkling*?

"Good morning, good morning, and a good day to all."

It was her father.

Margery closed her book and presented him with a heavily powdered cheek for her morning kiss. He patted Elly and Aggy on the head and bumbled over to the kitchen to wrap Cinders up in a great big bear hug.

"And a special good morning to you, my little princess," he said, pushing his spectacles all the way up on his nose. "On dish duty again, are we? Whatever did you do this time?"

"Nothing," she replied, sticking her suspiciously sparkly hands deep in the pockets of her apron. "Honest."

"She set the kitchen rug on fire, left my riding boots out in the rain, and Agnes caught her feeding her vegetables to the dog," Margery corrected.

"Did he like the vegetables?" her father asked.

"I think he would have preferred sausages," Cinders replied.

"Me too," he agreed.

Margery sighed. Cinders smiled.

"Well, well, well, I have a very busy day ahead of me," her father announced. "If the king wants to throw a ball, he's going to need a ballroom, and most ballrooms, as I understand it, have a roof."

"It is traditional," Margery agreed.

Cinders's father was the royal builder. Every day, he left their little pink cottage and traveled through the woods all the way to the palace. At night he would show Cinders his plans and sketches for towers and turrets, but she was never allowed to accompany her father into town. She dreamed of seeing the palace he had built for King Picklebottom, the place where her mother and father had met.

"If you left off the roof, we could dance under the stars." Cinders twirled in a perfect pirouette and immediately crashed into a stack of tea towels.

"You won't be dancing under anything," Agnes said. "I hardly think the prince would invite someone like you to the ball."

Cinders looked down at her stained, ragged dress, then over at her sisters with their glossy brown hair, painstakingly applied makeup, and gorgeous, grown-up gowns. All before 9 a.m. on a Wednesday.

"We'll make a lady out of Cinders yet,"

her father said, planting a kiss on the top of her head. "She is my little princess, after all."

Aggy and Elly pretended to stick their fingers down their throats before turning on sweet smiles for their stepfather.

"Do you think I might be able to go to the ball this time?" Cinders asked her father. "I'd love to see the palace."

"Not this time, little one," he replied with a sad smile. "Maybe next year."

He always said that.

"You always say that," she said. "Aggy's been to the palace. Elly's been to the palace. Why can't I go?"

She planted her hands on her hips and fixed her father with her most serious stare.

"Oh, Cinders," he said with a sigh. "You just have to trust me. You'll get to the palace one day, just not yet."

It was the same story every time she asked—he always had a reason not to take her: there wasn't room in his carriage; she wouldn't like the food they served; everyone was far too busy to show her around. If she didn't know better, she'd think her father was trying to keep her away from the palace altogether.

"Fine. I'm going outside to feed Sparks," she said quickly, hugging her father goodbye and running outside before her stepmother could stop her. "But you'd better take me next time!"

Chapter Two

SLAMMING THE BACK DOOR behind her, Cinders ran down the garden and cut into the forest as fast as her legs would carry her, until her father, her stepsisters, her stepmother, and her dashed dreams of attending the king's ball were left far, far behind. Sparks, her big red fluffy dog, leaped to his feet and hurtled after his best friend. Once she was far enough away from the cottage, she plopped down onto the soft ground and examined her hands. Not a trace of sparkles, not even the slightest suggestion of fizziness.

"What was all that about?" she muttered to no one in particular.

"I'm sure I don't know," replied a snooty voice. "Could it possibly have had anything to do with sausages?"

Cinders jumped up and looked all around. "Who said that?" But there was no one to be seen.

"I don't mean to harp on, but I'm terribly hungry. I haven't had any breakfast yet, you see. I don't suppose you've got anything in your pockets? A frankfurter? A hot dog? Even a chipolata would do the trick."

Cinders blinked and rubbed her eyes. If she

didn't know better, she might have thought Sparks was the one talking.

"Brilliant," she said with a big sigh. "I've gone mad. First I'm imagining flying dishes, and now a talking dog."

Sparks wagged his large, shaggy tail.

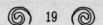

"What's so mad about that?" he asked. "A talking dog is a lot more sensible than leaving the house without so much as a single sausage, if you ask me."

"You're talking!" Cinders yelled.

"Clearly," Sparks replied.

"But dogs can't talk!" she shouted.

"Well, I can," he said.

"Everything all right over there?"

Cinders looked up to see her neighbors, Jack and Jill, walking toward her. Sparks stuck out his tongue and panted happily.

"Oh, yes," she said, keeping one eye on her dog. "Although I'm starting to think I might have bumped my head in the night."

"Nasty business that," Jack said, pointing to his own bandaged noggin. "You want to be careful."

"Try wrapping it up with some vinegar and brown paper," Jill suggested. "That always works for us."

"Thanks," Cinders said, waving them off as they disappeared down the path. "I'll do that."

"Vinegar also happens to go very nicely with fries, which go even better with sausages," Sparks commented, making his friend jump. "Just a suggestion I'm putting out there."

Cinders stared at the big red dog in front of her. "You can talk," she whispered.

"Apparently so," he replied in a woofy-yet-dignified voice.

"But you've been mine since I was a baby," Cinders said. "How come you've only just started talking today?"

"Never really felt like it before," he said,

scratching his ear with a hind leg. "To be honest, most of the things you lot talk about are very dull. *Ooh*, the prince has got a new cape. *Ooh*, they've painted the castle blue. *Ooh*, it's raining—no it's not, yes it is. *Blah-blah-blah*."

"Well, there's no need to be rude," Cinders replied, looking at her hands again. If Sparks really was talking, perhaps those dishes really did fly into the sink earlier. Or maybe she really had hit her head. "I wish there was someone who could explain what's going on."

"Maybe there is," Sparks said with a wink. "Though *I* wish we had some sausages."

"Me too." Cinders rubbed her hand against her rumbling tummy. "I wish we had a whole plateful of sausages."

Before she could even blink, her hands began to tingle and a giant platter, piled high with plump pork sausages, appeared in front of them.

"Whatever you just did," Sparks said as he dived toward the pile of sausages, "please do it again."

"What is going on?" Cinders demanded, waving her glittery hands in the air. "I wish everything would just stop for a moment!"

And everything did.

Everything and everyone was silent and

still. Sparks was frozen in midair, a family of bluebirds hovered overhead, and a pair of butterflies hung happily in the sky as though time had stopped completely.

"Oh, dear me," Cinders said. "This can't be good."

Chapter Three

"**H**ELLO?" **CINDERS WAVED A** glittering hand in front of Sparks's face. He didn't move. She clicked her fingers up at the bluebirds, but they just stayed exactly where they were, floating right above her head.

"Oh, dear me indeed," she said again. "This isn't good at *all*."

"I don't know . . . it's nice to have a bit of peace and quiet sometimes, isn't it?"

A tiny red-haired woman appeared as if from nowhere. She gave Cinders a little wave and snagged some sausages from the plate in front of Sparks's nose, munching away happily while Cinders stared. Like most people with at least one half-decent parent, she had been brought up not to stare, but it was hard not to gawk at this woman. Her hair was nearly the exact same shade of red as Sparks's fur, and her skin was so pale that it almost glittered. She was a very stare-at-able person.

And that was before you even considered the fact that she had a pair of wings sprouting out of her back.

And was floating.

In the air.

"Okay, someone's going to have to tell

me what's going on," Cinders said, looking her new friend up and down, from her big black boots and bright blue tutu to the floppy purple bow in her hair.

"Cinders, is it?" the flying woman asked. Cinders nodded.

"Brilliant." She finished off a sausage and licked her fingers before starting on another. "Having a difficult day?"

"You could say that," Cinders said. She wrapped her arms around Sparks, trying to pull him back down to the ground, but he wouldn't budge. "Don't suppose you've got any idea what's going on?"

"I could hazard a guess." The woman looked up at the floating dog. "Magic isn't always terribly reliable, especially when you're just starting out."

"Magic?"

Cinders let go of Sparks and looked down at her fingers.

"What else did you think was going on?" The little pale lady held out her hand. "Hello, I'm your godmother."

Remembering her manners, Cinders took the hand in her own and her skin began to tingle again. "I think you might have the wrong person," she said. "I haven't got a godmother."

"Actually, you have"—the woman fluttered her wings—"because I'm it. I realize I'm a bit late, but in my defense, you were very difficult to find. You're not on any kind of social media, are you? What's that all about? Oh, I should have introduced myself properly—you can call me Brian."

Cinders looked down and realized she was still shaking the woman's hand.

"Where I'm from, Brian is generally considered a man's name," she said as politely as possible, letting go of Brian's hand.

"Says who?" Brian replied. "It's a perfectly good name. Why on earth would you stop half the people on the planet from using it?"

"Beats me," Cinders said. "That's just how it is."

Brian shook her head in disagreement. "You make no sense, you people. Doesn't really matter, does it? I do love the way it rolls off the tongue."

To be fair, Cinders couldn't really argue with her.

"Anyway, I'm not sure you'd be able to pronounce my real name," Brian went on. "So let's stick with Brian for now. I'm guessing you've got some questions."

"One or two." Cinders nodded. "Mostly about the whole magic thing. And the godmother thing. And the talking dog. And the wings."

"The last one is easy. I need the wings to

fly," Brian replied, speaking very clearly, as if Cinders might not understand. "And I'm your godmother because your mother chose me to be your godmother. That's usually how that works. As for the magic, I don't know why it's decided to show itself today, but if you want to tell me what you've been up to, that might give me a clue."

"You knew my mother!" Cinders's eyes opened wide. "Oh my goodness, please can you tell me about her?" Whenever she asked her father about her mother, he went all quiet and got a faraway look in his eyes.

"I can." Brian nodded. "But shouldn't we get your dog back on the ground first?"

"I suppose we should," Cinders agreed. "I don't know what happened. One minute he was just an ordinary dog and the next he started talking. Then I wished things would stop for a moment and everything froze."

"Ah, there you have it," Brian said with a wise smile. "You made a wish. Wishes are very powerful, you know."

"I wished for the sausages as well," Cinders said slowly. "And I wished that the dishes would do themselves. Are you telling me I can grant my own wishes?"

"Who else do you expect to grant them?" Brian asked. "I might be a fairy, but I've got far better things to do with my day than produce a plate of sausages out of thin air every time someone clicks their fingers. Although, that said, these are very tasty sausages."

"You're a fairy?" Cinders asked, saucer-eyed.

Brian fluttered her wings. "These things

didn't give it away? You know your mom was a lot cleverer than you."

"And you really knew my mother?"

"You could say that," Brian replied, turning a somersault in midair. "You look a lot like her, you know."

Other than her father, Cinders had never, ever met anyone who had known her mother, and every time she asked her father to tell her a story about their life together, he looked so sad she couldn't stand it. Brian was the first person she'd ever met who had so much as *heard* of her mother, and she was a real-life, flying fairy.

Cinders really needed a little sit-down.

"I've never met a fairy before," she said slowly. "I didn't think they were real. I mean, I know there are elves, and I met an exceptionally disagreeable troll who lives under the bridge once upon a time, but I thought fairies were ... well. From fairy tales."

Brian looked slightly concerned. "I *think* I'm real," she replied. "At least I'd better be. I've left the oven on at home and there'll be hell to pay if I accidentally burn the house down."

Brian, Cinders decided, was definitely real.

"Any more questions?" her fairy godmother asked. "I haven't got all day, you know."

"How do we get him back on the ground?" Cinders asked, turning her attention to Sparks. Her stepmother had been furious when she shrank her favorite sweater in the wash, and she would not be happy if Cinders left the dog hanging around in midair.

"Wishes are tricky things," Brian said. "Sometimes they stick; sometimes they don't. Depends how much you mean it when you make the wish. Your magic definitely isn't all there yet, so if you can wait until midnight, the spell should undo itself. Magic always runs out at midnight."

"I think we should try to get him down before then," Cinders said, patting his big red head. "This is literally the worst day for him to start talking. I'm never going to hear the end of it."

"As your magic grows, you'll have more control over it," Brian promised, helping herself to more sausages. "But while you're learning, you'll have to speak your wishes out loud. And they must be very, very specific wishes, otherwise, well, I don't need to tell you what could happen." Brian waved her hand at the frozen bluebirds and the flying dog.

"All I have to do is make a wish?" Cinders asked.

Brian the fairy gave a nod.

"I wish things would go back to normal," Cinders said.

Her fingertips started to sparkle, then glow, and in the blink of an eye, the birds began singing, the butterflies flapped away into the sky, and Sparks dived face-first into the now-empty plate of sausages.

"All right, someone's got some explaining to do," he grunted, rubbing his snout with a paw. "Who is this? What's going on?"

"I think the first thing you need to do is have a chat with those two," Brian said, pointing across the clearing to where Aggy and Elly were staring, slack-jawed, at Cinders, Sparks, and her fairy godmother.

"Oh, good grief." Cinders clapped a hand across her forehead as Elly grabbed her sister's hand and legged it back through the forest. "I'd better try to explain before they tell my stepmother what they saw. Will you wait here, um, Brian?"

"No," said Brian with a big, cheery smile. "But I will see you later. Now get back home before the messenger leaves."

With that, she vanished.

"Messenger?" Cinders said to Sparks. "What is she talking about?"

"Haven't the foggiest," Sparks replied, "but can you please explain one thing?"

"I can try." Cinders sighed. "It's all a bit complicated, isn't it? What with the magic, the fairy godmother, and you talking all of a sudden."

"Who cares about any of that?" Sparks gestured at the empty plate. "What on earth happened to all my sausages?"

Chapter Four

AT THE EXACT SAME time as Cinders and Sparks arrived back at the cottage, a short man on a tall horse galloped away, tooting on a horn as he went.

"That must be the messenger Brian was talking about," said Sparks. "Did you see the royal crest on his cloak?"

"That's the least of my problems," Cinders replied. "What do you think Elly and Aggy saw in the forest?"

As it turned out, Elly and Aggy had seen everything.

"And there was a lady with red hair and she had wings!" Aggy wailed as Cinders walked into the cottage with Sparks close behind. "And Sparks was floating!"

Closing her eyes and crossing her fingers, Cinders prepared herself for the worst. But Margery didn't say a thing. When Cinders opened her eyes, she saw that her stepmother was far too busy reading a golden scroll to listen to her daughters.

"And then the lady with the wings disappeared!" Aggy squealed. "*Poof*—just like that!"

"Agnes, I do not have time to listen to your nonsense," Margery announced. "And I've told you before, I won't have you telling lies."

"But it's not a lie," Aggy said sulkily. "There was a lady with wings and Sparks was flying and—"

"Enough!" snapped her mother, waving the scroll in the air. "Can any of you guess what this scroll says?"

Aggy and Elly shook their heads.

"Obviously not," Cinders replied, breathing a sigh of relief. "Who sends scrolls anymore? Why wouldn't they send you a DM like normal people?"

"Because it isn't from *normal* people," Margery replied. "This is from the palace. It's an invitation to the king's ball, the most fabulous party the palace has ever thrown."

Elly and Aggy forgot all about Brian as soon as they heard the word "ball."

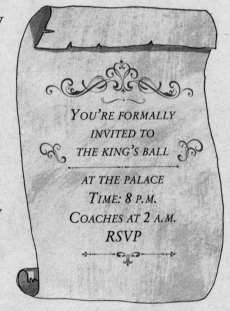

YOU'RE FORMALLY INVITED TO THE KING'S BALL

*AT THE PALACE
TIME: 8 P.M.
COACHES AT 2 A.M.
RSVP*

"Will we have new dresses, Mother?" asked Elly.

Margery nodded.

"And new shoes?" asked Aggy.

Margery nodded.

"Can I go too?" asked Cinders.

"Certainly not," replied Margery. "Your name isn't on the invitation, so you're not invited. And I don't want to hear another word on the matter. Now, haven't you got chores to do?"

Of course the answer was yes. Cinders *always* had chores to do.

Chapter Five

A **WHOLE WEEK WENT BY** and Cinders hadn't
been able to make a single wish come
true.

Every morning, she woke up and did all her
jobs: she washed the dishes, fed the animals, and
polished her stepsisters' shoes until she could
see her own sad face reflected in the super-shiny
leather. She hadn't teased Elly or Aggy, she
hadn't talked back to her stepmother, and she
hadn't eaten a single cake all week long. Once

the whole cottage was spick-and-span, Cinders snuck out of the house and into the forest with Sparks at her side, where they spent each and every day wishing and wishing and wishing for Brian to come back and tell Cinders more about her mother.

But nothing happened.

"Maybe you're not magic after all," Sparks suggested, merrily chewing on a sausage he had yanked from the kitchen. "Maybe it was all a dream."

"Says Sparks the Talking Dog," Cinders replied. She lay down on the grass and stared up at the cloudless sky. "I don't understand why none of my wishes are coming true anymore. My fairy godmother hasn't been back, and I don't even get to go to the ball tonight. Everything's just so terrible."

"Sounds grand to me," Sparks said. "Nice empty house, no one yapping on while I'm trying to take a nap."

"Weren't you the one who woke everyone up this morning?" Cinders asked with a stern look. "Barking at a squirrel?"

"That squirrel was quite clearly trying to break into the house and steal all the cookies," he replied, his fluffy red fur standing on end. "I was merely protecting the family."

"Whatever." Cinders sighed. "I just really, really, really want to see the palace. You know that's where my mom and dad met?"

Sparks sat up straight. "Then go," he said. "What's stopping you?"

Cinders shook her head at her silly friend. He might be able to talk, but he was no genius.

"I haven't got a dress," she explained with

her eyes closed. "Or a carriage. Or a horse to pull the carriage. Or a footman to take care of the horses I haven't got to pull my nonexistent carriage."

Cinders stretched out in the grass and imagined how beautiful the palace must look. Even though she'd never seen it, she dreamed about it all the time, and her father often sat with her in her room, telling her tales of the white marble staircase and tall white towers with turrets that stretched up high into the sky. Tonight it would be at its most fabulous, all lit up with candles, music playing, people dancing and, in the middle of it all, her father, proudly showing off the new ballroom he had built for this very occasion.

"Perhaps your wishes haven't been working because you weren't wishing for things you really, really wanted," Sparks suggested after a quiet moment. "When do your stepsisters leave for the palace?"

"Margery said the carriage was leaving after lunch." Cinders opened one eye. The sun was high in the sky and her tummy was rumbling. Lunchtime must have been hours ago. "Why?"

"Let's go home," he suggested,

"and see

what we

can see."

Chapter Six

THE LITTLE PINK COTTAGE was as quiet as a mouse when they returned. Actually, it was as quiet as the two white mice Cinders and Sparks saw running to hide behind the sofa when they opened the door.

"Right, we need a dress, a carriage, and two horses," Sparks said, kicking the door closed with his back legs while Cinders grabbed half a leftover doughnut from the kitchen worktop and gobbled it up in two big bites. "There's no fairy godmother here to conjure those up, so what are you going to do?"

"I've waited my whole life to go to the palace, and today's the day. If no one's going to help me, I'll just have to help myself," Cinders said, determined. She squeezed her hands into tight little fists, scrunched up her face, and concentrated as hard as she possibly could. "I wish I had a ball gown of my very own."

At first the fizzing feeling was very faint. Just a tiny tickling in the tippity-tips of her fingers. Then it began to grow. Her whole hand started to glimmer and gleam and suddenly Cinders's entire body was covered in gold sparkles.

"Ooh, steady on," Sparks said, backing away and hiding under the settee.

"I think it's working!" Cinders shouted, spinning around and around and around.

"That or you're about to turn into a human fireworks display," Sparks called back. "Which would really be very inconvenient."

Slowly, the spinning stopped and the sparkles faded away.

"Did it work?" Cinders asked.

"I think it did," Sparks replied, his tongue hanging out of a big doggy smile.

"Good golly gosh," Cinders whispered as she turned to look in the mirror. "It most certainly did."

Instead of her usual rags, Cinders saw

something altogether different. Gone was the
messy girl with blueberry stains on her skirt
and her wild hair. Instead she was staring at
a fine young lady wearing a glorious gown.
At first it looked as though it had been spun

from silver silk, but every time she moved, the fabric shimmered with all the colors of the rainbow. Her hair was soft and curly and, for the first time in what felt like her entire life, she was spotlessly clean. Cinders had never seen herself look that way before. If she didn't know who she was, she wouldn't have even recognized herself.

"What do you think?" she asked Sparks, still stunned.

"I think you need to put something on your feet," he said, disappearing into the closet, his tail wagging behind him. "Let's see if these fit."

Sparks dropped a pair of beautiful shoes in front of his best friend. They looked as though they were made of glass and, just like the dress, they sparkled in the light, shining

with more colors than Cinders could name. She slipped them on and gasped with delight. A perfect fit!

"Wherever did these come from?" she asked, tapping and turning in her new shoes. It felt as though they'd been made just for her.

"They were your mother's," Sparks replied, still smiling. "I'd have given them to you before, but glass slippers don't really go with rags."

She couldn't be sure, but Cinders was fairly certain she could feel the same magical tingle in her toes as soon as she slipped on the shoes.

"Come on, then," Sparks said. "We're not done yet. We still need a carriage, horses, and a footman, and we haven't got all day."

"Hmm . . ." Cinders took a deep breath and closed her eyes. She really, really, really wanted to go to the ball. "I wish I had a carriage and a horse and a footman."

"Two horses!" Sparks corrected. "Or you'll be riding around in circles."

"Two horses!" Cinders agreed as the tingling began again. "Ooh, here we go!"

As the sparkles began to surround her, she felt herself spinning around and around and around again.

"Oh, no!" Sparks yelped. "Cinders, make it stop!"

"Is everything all right?" she shouted. She couldn't see a thing.

"I should say not," Sparks replied as the spinning and sparkles subsided.

Once she had steadied herself, Cinders opened her eyes and gasped. A short, stout, red-headed man with big brown eyes stood in the center of the room, dressed in a red satin suit, wearing a very familiar leather collar.

"*Sparks?*" Cinders asked.

"The utter indignity," he muttered, brushing off his spotless sleeves. "However am I supposed to stay up on my hind legs all night long? And would you look at those poor mice?"

Cinders turned to see two tall speckled

horses standing in the middle of the kitchen.

"They've still got their whiskers," she said, grabbing two sugar lumps from the tea tray and offering them to her new four-legged friends. They both shook their heads, whinnying in disgust. Thinking fast, Cinders grabbed a big block of cheese from the cupboard, chopped it in half, and held out her hands. The horse-mice gobbled it up in two seconds flat.

"Well," she said, sighing, "I suppose I am still learning."

"Yes," Sparks agreed as he pushed past her to open the door. "I suppose you are. And don't forget we have to be back before midnight—Brian said magic always runs out at midnight." He began leading the way to the carriage.

As he went, Cinders noticed a bright red bushy tail poking out from the back of his trousers.

"Oh, dear," she said, pushing her horse-mice through the kitchen door and out toward the huge crystal carriage waiting for them in the yard. "Maybe this isn't such a good idea."

"Too late to change your mind now," Sparks replied, wagging his tail.

"Off to the palace we go!"

Chapter Seven

"**W**OW," CINDERS GASPED WHEN they pulled up in front of the palace. "It's flipping enormous."

"It's a palace," Sparks replied. "They tend to be rather on the large side. Hmm, now, can you smell that? I bet the sausages here are out of this world."

Cinders climbed down from her crystal carriage as gracefully as possible (which wasn't very graceful at all) and gasped again. The palace really was a sight to see. She thought it might be bigger than her entire village, and the six shining white turrets stretched all the way up into the sky. Music poured out of every window, and Cinders found herself swaying back and forth as her two horse-mice squeaked along in time to the tune.

"Excuse me, milady."

She looked up to see a tall guard, wearing an incredibly elaborate hat, staring down at her.

"Me?" Cinders asked. For a moment, she had completely forgotten what she was wearing and why she was there. She loved music so much and never heard it at home. Anything even approaching a tune gave her stepmother a headache.

"Yes, milady," he replied. "I'm going to need you to move your carriage."

"Right," Cinders agreed, straightening her shoulders and clearing her throat. "Footman, take the carriage and the horses, ah, wherever one takes carriages and horses."

"At once, modom," Sparks the footman said with a very doggy-like growl.

"One will be inside eating as many sausages as one can get one's hands on," she said. "Perhaps one will be able to bring you, um, one."

The palace guard gave her a funny look before waving her toward what looked like an endless marble staircase that led into the palace.

"Have fun," Sparks replied with a wink and what sounded like a woof as she tottered away in her mother's glass slippers. "And remember, **WE HAVE TO BE HOME BEFORE MIDNIGHT!**"

When she finally made it all the way to the top of the staircase, Cinders couldn't believe her eyes. Just as her father had promised, there was a glorious new ceiling above the ballroom, painted to look exactly like the night sky, and studded with diamonds to show where the stars should be.

Everything was so grand and everyone was so fancy that it looked as if one of her sisters' celebrity magazines had come to life. Cinders had never seen so many colorful gowns or powdered wigs. Come to think of it, she'd never actually seen a powdered wig before.

Almost everyone in the room was wearing what looked like a bright white hat made out of hair. The only people without such a silly thing seemed to be the servants, and they didn't look very happy at all.

"I wish I had a powdered wig," Cinders whispered under her breath. For a second, she felt a faint tingle in her fingertips, followed by something prickly. She looked down and saw a tiny tree branch covered in flour.

"I said a *powdered wig*, not a *powdery twig*," she muttered as her cheeks began to flush with embarrassment. Would everyone be able to tell she didn't belong? All she wanted to do was dance and sing and find a plate of sausages for Sparks, but instead she hovered by the entrance to the ballroom, too afraid to join in. Maybe her family was right—maybe she didn't belong at the palace after all.

"Perhaps I should find something to eat," she said to herself, throwing away the twig and rubbing her grumbling tummy. "I always feel better after a snack."

And—oh—what snacks she found!

The palace cooks had prepared the most incredible-looking feast Cinders had ever seen. Roast suckling pigs, enormous turkey legs, tureens of soup, baskets full of bread, and platter after platter piled with candied fruit, cakes, cookies, sweets, and the biggest wibbly-wobbly Jell-O molds in the world.

For seven long days, Cinders hadn't so much as looked at anything sweet. She'd been on her very best behavior ever since she'd found out about her fairy godmother, and in her stepmother's house very best behavior meant absolutely no sweet treats. But Cinders had an uncontrollable sweet tooth, especially for cake, and now, standing in front of the dessert table, she was powerless to resist.

"Maybe just one little slice," she said, grabbing a plate and reaching across the table for the slightest sliver of chocolate gateau. "And just half a cookie. And maybe some of these little Jell-O things. And I really would like to try the chocolate pudding . . ."

Before she knew it, Cinders's plate was piled so high she could barely manage to carry it.

Hmm. Now, where to sit?

There were a dozen or so tables on the other side of the feast, covered in crisp white cloths,

where she spotted some of the powdered-wig wearers tucking in to their dinner.

"Excuse me," she said, approaching a tall, skinny man with a ginger mustache, who was eating alone at one of the tables. "Is anyone sitting here?"

"All these seats are taken," he replied without even looking at Cinders.

"But there's no one else here." She glanced around the empty table, confused.

"All these seats are taken," he said again.

"Must be rough having all those friends," she muttered as she walked away, shaking her head. Taking a deep breath, Cinders moved on to the next table. Five of the seats were filled with girls about her own age, but one remained enticingly empty.

"Hello," Cinders said, straining under the weight of her groaning plate. "Is anyone sitting here?"

"No," replied one of the girls. Cinders couldn't help but notice they all looked almost exactly alike. The same powdered wig, the same bright blue lipstick, and nearly identical ball gowns, all in slightly different shades of pink. "Do sit down."

"Thanks!"

Cinders pulled out the chair and sat down. To her surprise, something moved under the table, something warm and furry, tickling her leg. She looked under the tablecloth.

No, not furry. Woolly.

Under the table were a number of sheep, with bows tied in their wool.

"Um . . ." she said. "There are sheep under the table."

"Oh, yes, those are mine," said the girl who had invited her to sit down. "I'm Bo Peep. I never go anywhere without my sheep, not since I lost them once."

"Oh . . ." said Cinders. "Right."

She began eating her treats. She'd never tasted anything so glorious in all her life! Only when she was halfway through her plate. did she realize that all five girls were staring at her.

"Would you like a cookie?" she asked, reluctantly pushing her plate toward them.

"Oh, no!" said Bo Peep. "We only eat greens."

"We only eat greens," echoed one of the other girls, and another nodded.

"Where on earth did you get that dress?" Bo Peep asked.

"I made it," Cinders replied, looking down at her beautiful gown. It was more or less true after all. "Where did you get yours?"

"We all got ours from Monsieur Couture, of course," the second girl said. "Everyone gets their dresses from Monsieur Couture."

"Ah." Cinders nodded. "That explains why they all look the same . . . um . . . same kind of lovely. They're very nice. I like all the ruffles."

In truth, Cinders did not like the ruffles— there were far too many of them. You could, after all, have too much of a good thing.

"Why aren't you wearing a hairpiece?" the third girl asked.

"You mean a wig?" Cinders gestured toward their matching hairdos. "Um, I must have left mine in my carriage. Silly me."

"You've got chocolate cake on your face," the fourth girl said.

"Saving it for later," Cinders muttered, swiping at her cheek with a napkin.

"Maybe you should sit somewhere else," the fifth girl suggested.

"Maybe I should," Cinders agreed, jumping to her feet and picking up her plate of desserts. "Have a lovely evening, everyone."

Struggling to keep a smile on her face, Cinders trotted away from the table and looked for somewhere else to sit. Who wanted to spend the evening with such boring people anyway? If she wanted to sit around, not eat sweets, and talk about fancy dresses all evening, she could stay home with her stepsisters. Plus, they all looked the same. *Bo Peep and her sheep*, she thought to herself.

After all that effort, the ball was a bust.

Even though she could see people dancing and eating, no one looked as if they were truly enjoying themselves. There was no laughter, no singing, and the musicians were struggling to play in their tight, high collars and big, heavy wigs. At the farthest end of the ballroom, Cinders saw three thrones. Right in the middle, perched on the biggest throne, sat the king. He was a shortish, grayish, grumpy-looking man who was sulking in the middle of the biggest party his kingdom had seen in years. To his right was the queen. She was also shortish, grayish, and grumpy-looking, which made her slightly askew powdered wig and ruffled rose-pink gown look really quite silly. The throne to the left of the king was empty.

"Should have sat there," Cinders said, nibbling on some nougat. "I wonder where the prince is."

Still holding her incredibly heavy plate, Cinders glanced around the room, looking for a place to sit. Just when she was about to give up and go home, she spotted a pair of legs disappearing under a table laden with salads and vegetables. Strangely enough, now that Bo Peep's crowd had eaten, no one seemed to be too bothered about the salad station. Trying not to draw attention to herself, Cinders sidled over to the veggies and stuck her head underneath the heavy tablecloth.

A boy with a crown on his head and cake all over his face stared back at her.

"Hello." Cinders put her plate on the floor and clambered under the table. No easy task in a ball gown. "Who are you hiding from?"

"Everyone?" the boy replied. "Hello, I'm Prince Joderick."

Chapter Eight

CINDERS HELD OUT HER hand and, after a moment's consideration, Prince Joderick shook it.

"I'm Cinderella, but everyone calls me Cinders," she said.

"Why?" the prince asked.

"I don't know," Cinders replied. "Cinderella is a bit of a mouthful, isn't it?"

"No one calls me Jodders," the prince said,

furrowing his brow. "And Joderick Jorenson Picklebottom is much worse than Cinderella."

"Probably because you're a prince and I most certainly am not a princess," she said. "Thank goodness."

Prince Joderick looked surprised. "You don't want to be a princess?" he asked.

Cinders shook her head while shoveling a huge brownie into her mouth. "No, thank you very much," she said. "Not if I'd have to live like this. I thought this was going to be a fun party, but everyone looks so miserable. I'd much rather live in my pink cottage in the forest where I can run around in the woods or play with my dog. Although, I have to say, the desserts here are top-notch."

The prince looked surprised, as if he wasn't used to people telling him what they really thought, but he rather liked it.

"I'm sorry," Cinders apologized. "I always say the wrong thing when I'm nervous."

"Don't be sorry," the prince said. "And you shouldn't be nervous—I'm the one who's hiding under a table after all."

"Why *are* you hiding from everyone?" Cinders asked. It did seem a little off when she thought about it.

"My father threw this party so I could choose someone to marry," Joderick explained. Cinders almost choked on her brownie. Aggy and Elly would be beside themselves. "But I'd much rather be riding my horse or playing video games or baking."

"Baking?" Now he was talking.

"I made those brownies." Prince Joderick nodded at Cinders's plate. "I'm a pretty good baker, but my dad doesn't like me to do it. He says that's Cook's job."

Cinders considered this for a moment while she chewed another brownie. "Controversial thought, but have you ever considered telling your dad to take a hike?" she asked. "Because you really shouldn't waste your time getting married when you could be in the kitchen knocking out another batch of these wonderful things."

"No one tells my father what to do," Joderick gasped. He marveled at the brave girl in front of him, currently devouring her third brownie. "He's the king."

Cinders shrugged. "Seems to me you need to learn how to stand up for yourself," she said, thinking about her stepmother. It also seemed to her that she and Joderick had a lot in common. "You shouldn't have to do things you don't want to do."

"I think I will have to get married eventually," Joderick said. "Everyone does, don't they?"

Cinders shook her head. "I don't think it's the law, but if you're dead set on it I've got two sisters who would both love to marry you."

The prince perked up a little. "Really? Are they anything like you?" he asked.

"No," Cinders replied sadly. "Not at all."

For a while, the two new friends carried on eating their cakes in silence.

"I'm going to have to go back out there in a moment," Joderick said, pushing away his empty plate and wiping his face on the sleeve of his jacket. "At midnight, I'm supposed to dance with the person I've chosen to marry."

"MIDNIGHT?" Cinders sat up so quickly she bonked her head on the table above them. "It's almost midnight?"

"It is," he confirmed before adding shyly,

"I don't suppose you'd like to dance with me, Cinders?"

"I'm very sorry, but I have to go." Cinders grabbed a couple of extra brownies and tucked them into the pockets of her dress—because all the best dresses have pockets—and scrambled out from underneath the table. "It was nice to meet you, Jodders!"

"Cinders, wait!" Joderick yelled as Cinders dashed away, only pausing to grab a handful of sausages as she went.

"*Cinders?*" A familiar voice echoed that of the prince.

Cinders froze. Smack bang in front of her were the two biggest powdered wigs and enormous pink gowns with the most ruffles she had seen all night.

Elly.

And Aggy.

"*Excusez-moi*," Cinders said, putting on a pretend accent and covering her face with her hands. "'Ave you seen *le prince*? I believe 'e is looking for someone to—'ow do you say?—wed."

"Someone to wed?" Both girls turned away from their stepsister without a second glance and scuttled off to hunt for Prince Joderick.

Cinders breathed out a sigh. Then she bolted out of the ballroom, ran along the hallway, and leaped all the way down the marble staircase to find Sparks the footman and her two horse-mice waiting with the crystal carriage. She jumped inside, face-first, and her ball gown blew up over her head, displaying her bloomers to the entire kingdom.

"Home, Sparks," she sighed from underneath

her skirts as the palace clock began to chime.
"And don't spare the horses."

"There's no way we can get home before
midnight," Sparks replied. Cinders looked up

to see his red hair slowly transforming into a pair of silly shaggy ears as the palace clock chimed again. "And will you just look at your so-called horses!"

Cinders stuck her head out of the carriage to see their thick braided tails change into long, pink mouse tails.

"No one will help me if I don't help myself," she whispered, squeezing her hands into fists. "I wish we were at home already."

This time, the magic came quickly. The sparkles showered the coach and, for a moment, everything was a blur. The next thing Cinders knew, her bottom hit the ground with a bump. She was outside her cottage, wearing her rags, one glass slipper on her foot and the other nowhere to be seen. Sparks sat in front of her, happily chewing the sausages she'd grabbed on her way out of the palace. One of her former horse-mice squeaked angrily before running away under the front door of the house.

"Thank goodness for that," she said, picking herself up and dusting herself off. "Everything's back to normal."

"Not quite everything," Sparks said, still scoffing his sausages.

Cinders had turned two mice into horses, but only one had turned back into a mouse. The other stood in front of her, still very much a horse, but with shiny whiskers and a long pink tail.

"Oh," Cinders said.

"Squeak," replied the horse-mouse.

Chapter Nine

"**M**AYBE IT ISN'T QUITE midnight," Cinders suggested. "Maybe he'll change back at the stroke of twelve."

"Or maybe it's already five past," Sparks said, "and this is a bit of a magical hiccup."

"I should say." Cinders grabbed the horse-mouse's reins and led him into the stable. "I'm sorry, Mouse. I promise I'll find a way to fix you."

Mouse squeaked happily, flicked his tail,

and curled up in the corner of the stable as best he could. At least he didn't seem too upset about his predicament. Though he *was* trying to clean his whiskers with his hooves, which looked quite awkward.

"Tell me everything," Sparks insisted, following Cinders back across the garden and into the cottage. "Was it marvelous? Magnificent? Everything you've ever dreamed?"

"Actually, it was really boring," she told him. "Everyone was so prim and proper and no one was having fun. But I did meet the prince and he was okay."

"Who cares about the prince? I want to know about the food!" Sparks said. "Those sausages were the best I've ever had."

"The food was easily the best part," Cinders admitted, hugging her mother's shoe.

"Still, it was rather a fine adventure. Wait, did you see my other shoe outside?"

"I'll go and have a look," Sparks offered, wagging his tail all the way out the front door. "Sometimes your stepmother is right about you, Cinders. You don't know how to look after your things."

As the door slammed shut behind him, Cinders grabbed one of Aggy's pink dresses from the laundry pile, wrapped a white towel on top of her head, and began to twirl around the living room, singing to herself and holding her one remaining glass slipper high in the air.

"How do you do? I am Cinders, Princess of the Pink Cottage, and I only wear dresses with more ruffles than sense," she announced to her reflection. "And, don't you know, anyone who is anyone is covering their hair in talcum powder these days?"

While she was busy spinning around the room, she heard a commotion coming from outside the cottage.

"Sparks! What are you doing out at this hour? Cinders was supposed to lock you up in the basement before she went to bed."

It was her stepmother! And she was home far too early. That couldn't possibly be a good thing.

"The prince *definitely* said Cinders," Aggy said. "We heard him, Mama."

"The prince also refused to dance with anyone at the stroke of midnight, so there's quite clearly something wrong with him," Margery replied. "You must have misheard."

"The king seemed very angry," Elly added fretfully. "Do you think Prince Joderick will be in trouble?"

"He's in trouble with *me*," her mother replied. "Imagine sending everyone in the entire kingdom home early and without so much as a thank-you for coming. Frère Jacques came all the way from France! And for what? A couple of hours of dancing and a slice of subpar cake? I don't know, the prince has proven himself to be quite the spoiled young man."

Inside, Cinders wriggled out of Aggy's pink dress, threw the towel down on the floor, and ran as fast as she could to her tiny little cupboard of a bedroom, clutching her mother's glass slipper to her chest. The old wooden door stuck on its hinges, protesting with a loud creak as she tried her hardest to crack it open.

"Now, now, Margery," Cinders's father said as his keys jingle-jangled in the lock. "Prince Joderick is a fine young man. Imagine being presented with a room full of people you've never met and being told to pick one to live with for the rest of your life. That's not how love works, my dear."

"Who's talking about love?" Margery retorted. "I'm talking about marriage."

"You old romantic," Cinders's father chuckled. "Why don't you make us some hot chocolate while I go and check on my alleged little gate-crasher. And, for the record, I thought the cake was marvelous."

Beginning to panic, the gate-crasher in question pushed and *pushed* and *PUSHED* on the door, but it just wouldn't budge.

"I'm telling you, Mama," Aggy wailed, "the prince definitely said her name!"

"Then I'll be popping in to say goodnight to an empty bed," her father replied. "Don't be so silly, Agnes."

At that second, Cinders's door flew open and she hurled herself under the covers just in time for her father to poke his head into her room.

"There's my little princess," he said softly, leaning down to place a gentle kiss on her forehead. "I knew it. Thank goodness you weren't there this evening. What an absolute nightmare."

What a nightmare indeed, Cinders thought as she rolled over with a smile on her face.

Still holding her mother's shoe, she fell fast asleep to dreams of brownies and horse-mice and a night full **TO THE BRIM WITH ADVENTURE.**

Chapter Ten

BACK AT THE PALACE, Prince Joderick wasn't having nearly as nice a night as Cinders.

"It's a disgrace!" the king shouted, striding up and down the throne room.

"A disgrace," agreed the queen.

"You've made a mockery of the crown!" the king bellowed.

"A mockery," the queen echoed.

"The whole kingdom must be wondering what is wrong with you!" the king cried.

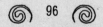

"The whole kingdom," the queen said with a sigh.

"If I might interrupt for just a sec," Joderick interrupted. "The thing is, I really didn't want to dance with anyone at the ball. They all just seemed a bit . . ." He paused and considered his mother's pink ruffled gown and enormous white wig. "They weren't for me."

"I really don't care," the king replied. "If you don't choose someone to marry by midsummer's eve, you'll have to marry the Princess of Fairyland, and then where will we be?"

"Where *will* we be?" the queen repeated.

"Hang on a minute." Joderick sat down slowly, scratching his head. "I'll have to marry who?"

The king took to his throne and removed

his crown, turning it around in his hands and inspecting the diamonds and rubies set within.

"Long ago, we were at war with the fairies and there was no way we could win," he explained. "They have terrible powers, my son—what wicked little things they are. All claws and teeth and spindly legs, obsessed with cakes and shiny things, and always using magic against us. But your clever great-great-grandfather made a pact with the King of Fairyland to get rid of them once and for all."

Joderick's eyes opened wide. Since he was a boy, his nannies and mannies had told him stories of the fairies, but he just thought they were making them up. He'd never seen a fairy and truly believed they didn't exist. In the stories he'd been told, fairies were tricksy, deceitful creatures. Legend said some of them could fly, some of them could disappear, and some of them had even been known to eat people. It was enough to make him long for a bowl of Brussels sprouts.

"Fairies are *real*?" Joderick asked, swallowing a lump in his throat.

"I'm afraid so," the king confirmed. "They agreed our lands could live in harmony provided the firstborn son of every king in this realm would marry a fairy of their choosing on midsummer's eve. Once the pact was made, the fairies were forbidden to cross beyond the Dark Mountains, and after a while, everyone in our kingdom forgot they were there."

"But you're not married to a fairy,"

Joderick pointed out. "And I'm fairly certain you're the first son of the first son of the first son of your great-grandfather."

"Actually, I'm the first son of the first son of the

second son," said the king. "My grandfather was a second son. His older brother married a fairy and was never seen again."

Joderick scratched his head, frowning, trying to figure out the family tree.

"Which is why you need to choose someone from this kingdom and you need to do it now," his father insisted. "There is a way out—as my own father discovered. If you're already married before midsummer's eve, then you don't have to marry one of those tricksy fairies."

"Oh, can you imagine?" The queen pressed her hand to her forehead. "What if one of them were to come and live in the palace? Or, even worse, you had to go and live in Fairyland?"

"And that's what *would* happen," the king confirmed as the queen began to sob. "As it did to my grandfather's brother, and his uncle before him. You would have to leave the kingdom and never, ever come back. You'd spend the rest of your life in the dark, dangerous place beyond the mountains and, let me tell you, no amount of horse riding could prepare you for a thing like that. It might not sound like it but Fairyland is a fearsome place, my son, and I won't let them take you away."

Joderick straightened his crown with a gulp. "When you put it like that, I suppose we'd better find me someone to marry." Clapping his hands together, the king leaped to his feet and two pages appeared instantly, carrying a very, very, very long scroll. And a laptop.

"This is a list of every eligible person who attended the ball," explained the king, logging on to the computer. "I've got their names and addresses and, on the scroll there, a humorous caricature, which, I must admit, was my idea." He chuckled. "Some of these are *very* good. Those ears!" He coughed. "Um. Anyway, my son, tell me. Who caught your eye this evening?"

The prince thought long and hard. He had met so many people that it was hard to remember them all. But there was one who had immediately sprung to mind.

"I didn't find out her last name," Joderick said slowly, "but I did meet a girl underneath the salad station."

"Oh, the scandal," the king gasped as the queen fainted.

"Her name was Cinders," Joderick added, pulling a glass slipper out of his rather large pocket.

"She left this behind when she disappeared. She was really funny and she liked my baking. I wouldn't mind marrying her."

"I really don't care!" the king whooped, and he waved to the pages who immediately began scanning the scroll for a Cinders. "As long as you're married by midsummer's eve and she's not a fairy, she's all right by me."

The prince looked on as his father scooped his mother up in his arms and began to dance her all around the throne room.

By this time tomorrow, Joderick would be engaged and the entire kingdom would rejoice.

So why wasn't he feeling happier about the whole situation?

Chapter Eleven

"**J**ODERICK, MY SON." THE king was exasperated. "Are you quite sure of the name?"

"Cinders." Joderick nodded. "Short for Cinderella."

The king, the prince, their royal guard, three dozen pages, and a hundred and one soldiers had been searching the length and breadth of the kingdom for three long days, and so far they'd found nothing.

They were riding through a clearing,

Joderick on a pony and his father on a magnificent charger. Beautiful sunlight dappled
the forest floor, yet there was nothing sunny
about the king's expression.

"But there isn't a single person in the land
called Cinders *or* Cinderella and, according to

our records, there never has been," the king said with a sigh. "Every baby born within my realm is required to be presented to the royal family and added to the register to stop any of those fanciful fairies from sneaking across our borders uninvited."

The horses stopped, and the king swung himself down from the saddle, kicking at the grass in frustration.

"She definitely wasn't a fairy," Joderick argued. "She didn't have wings, sharp fangs, or creepy claws. She was a real human girl."

"Then why haven't we found her?" the king said as his horse wandered off the track to drink at a stream. "And what kind of person loses a shoe? I'm starting to think you're making this girl up. It's almost as if you *want* to marry one of those terrible fairies."

Through the trees, Joderick spotted a thin wisp of smoke coming from a pink brick chimney.

He remembered what Cinders had said. *"My pink cottage in the forest . . ."*

"This way!" Joderick called, pulling his pony around and charging off through the trees. "I think I know where she is!"

Chapter Twelve

CINDERS, MEANWHILE, WAS SLOWLY making her way back from the well, with Sparks close at hand, when she heard all the commotion. She always took her time when bringing water back to the cottage. There were always interesting things to see in the woods and she was still hoping Brian might show her face again. Ever since the ball, Cinders hadn't been able to make a single wish come true, no matter how hard she tried.

Was Sparks right? Was it to do with how *hard* she wished? With how much she wanted the thing she was wishing for?

That didn't make sense, though, because she *really* wished Brian would come and explain this all, and it wasn't happening. Magic, it turned out, was complicated.

She slowed. The garden in front of the cottage was full of people. The yard behind the cottage was full of people. Some were wearing big black furry hats and others were wearing red-and-gold uniforms, and right in the middle were two men with crowns on top of their heads.

"Is it me," Sparks said, slowing down until he had almost stopped, "or does that look an awful lot like the king and Prince Joderick?"

"It does rather," Cinders agreed. "Whatever could they be doing at my house?"

"I'd like to say they've just stopped by to say hello, but that seems rather unlikely," he replied. "Maybe we should make a run for it."

But it was too late.

"There she is!"

Margery, eyes as wide as the dinner plates Cinders had not washed that morning, came running down the lane and grabbed her stepdaughter by the arm.

"We have her, Your Highness!" she bellowed to the king before leaning in to whisper in Cinders's ear. "Whatever you've been up to, you're in for it now, little miss."

"But I haven't done anything wrong," Cinders protested, not entirely sure it was true. Sparks kept close to her, growling as they approached the royal party.

"It's all right, my little princess," her father reassured her, even though from the look on his face things were far from all right.

"This is the one, is it?" the king said, eyeing her up and down. "The one you met at the ball? You're positive?"

"I think so," Joderick said, squinting at the messy girl with ratty hair. She did look really quite different from the girl he remembered.

"You'd better make sure," the king said, as clearly Joderick was not sure about this at all. "Because there are a lot of people in the kingdom, son. People who know how to wear clean clothes and curtsy to their king when he appears in their very own garden. Your mother tells me Belle broke up with the Beast, so she's available, but who knows for how long? Good-looking girl like that, decent pedigree, won't stay single."

Cinders felt a soft *bonk* on the top of her head.

"Curtsy," her stepmother ordered, a big, broad smile pasted across her face. "Now."

"But I can't curtsy," Cinders reminded her. "I always fall over."

"*Try*," Margery hissed.

"Can someone please explain what's going on?" Cinders asked as she folded herself over into a curtsy. "Why are you all here?"

Then she fell over. She picked herself up again, cheeks turning hot and red.

Prince Joderick hurried off to his horse and rummaged around in his saddlebag for a moment. When he turned around, he was holding something in his hands. Something small, pointy, and sparkly.

"My shoe!" Cinders gasped. Her missing glass slipper.

"She *was* at the ball," said Aggy.

"Oh, good detective work," said Margery sarcastically.

The prince held up the glass slipper. "I, Joderick Jorenson Picklebottom, crown prince of this realm, do declare that whomever this shoe should fit, will sit beside me on the throne."

Cinders stared at him, unimpressed.

"Um, you're supposed to try on the shoe," Joderick whispered to Cinders. "To find out if it's yours."

"But it's already mine," she replied. "I don't need to try it on. I know it fits."

"Yes, but you're supposed to try it on so everyone else can see," Joderick explained. "It was Mom's idea. To make it seem more exciting for the media, and less like you're just, um, a commoner. I mean, not that I think of you as a commoner. But you are. A commoner. Sorry. And then we can get married!"

Cinders stared at the assembled crowd. Elly and Aggy were glaring at their stepsister, her father was beaming with happiness, Margery's mouth hung open in shock, and the king, well, he appeared to be checking his elf phone.

A photographer hovered nearby, ready to get a shot of Cinders trying on the shoe.

"Can I not just have the shoe?" Cinders asked. "Without the married part?"

"Give it to me!" Margery yelled, grabbing the slipper and jamming it onto Cinders's bare foot. "Look! It fits! Yes! I'm going to be mother to a princess!"

"Stepmother," Aggy hissed.

"Hurray, yippee, etcetera," the king said.

"Pack up her things and get them to the palace. We've got a wedding to plan, pronto."

At once, Elly and Aggy burst into tears.

"But Cinders wasn't even supposed to be at the ball!" Aggy complained.

"And I don't want her to leave!" Elly whined.

But their mother couldn't have cared less. She had always dreamed of one of her daughters marrying the prince. All those riches, all those jewels. It was all she'd ever wanted. And as soon as Cinders was gone she was going to turn her room into a yoga studio.

"Don't pack up anything! I don't want to live in the palace," Cinders protested, hobbling away from the prince, one foot in a glass slipper. "I want to stay here with my dad."

"The prince can't very well come and live

here, can he?" the king replied, waving dismissively at the little pink cottage. "You haven't even got a moat."

"We'll build a moat!" Margery shrieked, apparently determined to see Cinders married off. "Elly! Aggy! Get digging!"

"Stop!" Cinders yelled as her sisters grabbed a pair of shovels. "You're not listening! I don't want to move to the palace and I don't want to marry the prince!"

One hundred soldiers, three dozen pages, the royal guard, Elly, Aggy, her father, her stepmother, and the king himself all gasped.

"What do you *mean* you don't want to marry the prince?" the king bellowed. "It's not a request—it's an order!"

"I know you didn't have a good time at the ball," Joderick said, getting down on one knee, "but it would be different if you lived at the palace. We'll have so much fun. And, when you're not in the mood for an adventure, you can read in the library or play on the grounds. Sometimes. When the grounds-keepers aren't around. And I'll bake you brownies every single day. You'll be so happy, Cinders, I promise."

Cinders considered this for a moment. They *were* very good brownies and Joderick was, as far as boys went, pretty okay. And when she really thought about it she couldn't help but feel that living at the palace would be an awfully big adventure.

"Dad"—she turned to face her father—"what do you think I should do?"

"You should do what feels right," he told her with a tear in his eye. "Your mother always wanted me to keep you away from the palace. Worried about you getting your head turned, or some such. But. Well. She's not here, is she?"

"No, she's not," said Cinders softly. She turned. "Would I have to wear a ball gown?" she asked Joderick.

"Sometimes," the prince replied, "but only on special occasions."

"Can I bring my dog?" she asked. "And my horse?"

"You most certainly can," the prince replied. "I love dogs and horses."

"And if you don't go," her stepmother said, smiling like a shark, "you'll have to stay here with me and do chores every day. In fact, I bet we could even think of some new ones to take your mind off making such a huge mistake."

"Can you give me two minutes to pack my bag?" Cinders asked the prince.

Joderick smiled, Margery clapped, and louder than ever, Elly and Aggy continued to cry.

"Now you're going to be *everyone's* princess," her father said, pulling her in for a big hug. "Just promise me you'll try to behave."

"I promise," she said, wiping away a tear.

"Speaking of which, any ideas why one of our horses keeps trying to nibble a hole in the stable wall? And squeaking?"

"Um, no, none," said Cinders.

Her dad narrowed his eyes, but they were sparkling. "I always knew you'd end up at the palace one day," he whispered. "Whatever your mom said. I only wish you didn't have to go just yet."

"Come along, ticktock," the king said, tapping his watch. "If we don't leave soon, I'm going to miss my TV show."

"Then let's go," Cinders said, putting on a big, brave smile.

"Probably not the best time to bring this up," Sparks whispered as Cinders made her way back into the pink cottage for the very last time, "but do you think you could speak to the prince and work a daily plate of sausages into the bargain?"

Chapter Thirteen

"**W**HAT I DON'T UNDERSTAND** is why she wasn't in the birth register in the first place," the king grumbled to the queen the very next morning. "There's no trace of the girl. It's as though someone has wiped away any record of her existence."

"Her father says the girl's mother brought her to the palace to register her when she was born," the queen said, taking her seat at the long golden table in the royal dining room, "but I don't remember it at all."

The king nodded. "The oddest thing is, there's no record of the mother either."

"Good morning, Father. Good morning, Mother," Joderick sang as he arrived for breakfast. He took his seat at the opposite end of the very long table and grinned a toothy grin. "How are you both this morning?"

"Hungry," his father replied.

"Famished," his mother added.

"Excellent," Joderick said. "What an exciting day."

The king looked at the queen and the queen looked at the king while Joderick filled his plate. This Cinders girl might not have been their first choice for a daughter-in-law, but their son was happy and soon he would be married, which meant the fairies couldn't steal him away.

And that was all that mattered.

WASN'T IT?

Chapter Fourteen

TWO TOWERS OVER, AND ten floors up, Cinders was in a considerably less chipper mood than the prince. They had arrived at the palace very, very late the night before and the king had sent everyone straight to bed. Even since she'd awoken, she'd had a very funny feeling in the pit of her stomach—a feeling that, for the first time, wasn't just a craving for pancakes.

Cinders was homesick.

Somehow, all her old clothes had gotten lost on their way from the carriage to her new chambers, and yet her closets were full to overflowing. Her new wardrobe was bigger than her old bedroom and her new bedroom was bigger than her entire house, and when she opened up the heavy oak doors, she saw a rainbow of gorgeous gowns and silky skirts, billowing blouses, and frock upon frock upon frock upon frock. It was Elly's and Aggy's dream wardrobe, and Cinders's worst nightmare. Even though everything was beautiful, she couldn't see anything she would have chosen for herself; it was all big skirts and tiny corsets, clothes made for sitting and standing rather than running and playing.

And it wasn't just her clothes. Nothing Cinders had brought from the little pink

cottage had found its

way into her new room. None of her books,
none of her trinkets, not even her one-of-a-
kind, homemade hula-hoop. Everything in
her room was shiny and new. Lovely, in a
way, but it just didn't feel like home.

The other strange thing was how quiet

it was at the palace. There were literally hundreds of servants in the castle, but not a single one made a single sound. Even when Cinders was alone at night, lying in her huge four-poster bed, she was afraid to make so much as a squeak. The only sound she heard all night was the gruffle and growl of Sparks's sleepy snores.

"Anyone would think you'd be more grateful after I rescued you from the kennels," she muttered, shaking her head at Sparks, still fast asleep. It turned out the king was allergic to dogs and had insisted Sparks live outside with the other royal hounds, but one quick mission under the cover of darkness later and he was safely sleeping under Cinders's bed. Mouse the horse was in the stables because even though her rooms were pretty huge, even Cinders couldn't hide a fully grown horse behind the settee.

The royal grooms had looked pretty surprised when Cinders said he only ate cheese, though.

"Something tells me I shouldn't be making many wishes while I'm in the palace," she said to herself, walking across the room and counting her extra-long steps. One, two, three, four, five, six, seven, eight, nine, ten. Ten steps from the bed to the window. "I do hope Brian will be able to find me here."

"I don't know if that's such a good idea," Sparks said, yawning as he clambered out from underneath the bed. "They don't like dogs, they don't like hula-hoops—I really don't think they're going to be that keen on fairy godmothers."

"Maybe you're right," Cinders replied, staring out the window. "Sparks, do you think we've made a terrible mistake?"

"I think you should call down to the kitchen for breakfast," he said. "I'll let you know after I've eaten."

The view from the palace really was glorious. Cinders had never been up so high and, from her room, she could see all the way from the ocean in the east to the mountains in the west. The sea was magical—a sweeping, sparkling stretch of blue that went on as far as the eye could see—but the mountains were another story altogether. Three tall peaks reaching so high into the sky that they could almost have blocked out the sun. Cinders had seen other mountains in her storybooks at home, magnificent mountains with beautiful snowy peaks, but these were as black as night from top to bottom. Cinders thought they looked like teeth, biting into the kingdom.

And yet . . . there was something about them that almost seemed to . . . draw her to them. A part of her that wanted to head up into those heights, through the snow . . . explore the valleys and peaks and what lay on the other side.

But she *hated* hiking. It was a good way to

ruin being outside, as far as she was concerned.

"Sparks?"

"Cinders?"

"Do you know what's beyond the mountains?" she asked her furry friend. She simply couldn't stop staring at them.

"Nothing you need to worry about." Sparks stretched out his long front legs. "Now, how are you getting on with that breakfast?"

Before she could answer, there was a loud knock on her bedroom door.

"Just a second!" Cinders yelped, pushing Sparks back beneath the bed. "I'm coming!"

She opened the door to see five young women in what she recognized as servants' uniforms, waiting patiently.

"Good morning, miss," said the first with a low curtsy.

"Good morning," Cinders said, awkwardly curtsying back.

"Good morning," said the second with a low curtsy.

"Good morning," Cinders said, wobbling down again.

"Good morning," said the third with a low curtsy.

"Good morn— Oh, no!" Cinders yelped as she fell face-first onto the floor. She looked up to see all five women looking down at her.

"Good morning, miss," said the fourth with a low curtsy.

"Okay, enough of that," Cinders replied, getting to her feet and dusting herself off. "How can I help you?"

The five women looked confused.

"We're here to help you," the first said.

"We're your ladies-in-waiting. We're here to tend to your every need. Is there anything we can get you right now?"

"Breakfast," Sparks coughed from underneath the bed.

"Breakfast," Cinders repeated quickly. "I'd love some breakfast. Sausages preferably."

"Oh." The first girl looked at the second. "Princesses don't usually eat sausages for breakfast."

"This one does," Cinders replied. "More important, you haven't told me your names. What should I call you?"

The second girl looked at the third, the fourth girl looked to the fifth, and the first looked straight back at Cinders.

"None of the royal family have ever asked our names before," she whispered. "They just ring a bell when they need us."

"Well, that's very rude," Cinders said, surprised. She had assumed everyone in the royal family had impeccable manners. "I'd really rather know your names if we're going to be friends."

"I'm Andy," said the first girl with a smile. "And these are my sisters, Candy, Sandy, Mandy, and Tandy."

"Oh," said Cinders. "Yeah, I'll admit that might take me a while. Still, it's very nice to meet you all."

"And it's very nice to meet you," Andy replied. Or possibly Tandy. "The king asked his butler to tell a page to tell the housekeeper to tell us that he and Prince Joderick will be in diplomatic negotiations all day long, so you are to amuse yourself until dinnertime."

"Oh." Cinders felt the smile fall from her face. "Doesn't matter, I suppose. I'm good at taking care of myself."

"Let's get your day started," the servant girl said. "Candy will get your breakfast, Sandy will draw your bath, Mandy will prepare your outfit, Tandy will make your bed, and I will let the housekeeper know she can tell the page to tell the butler to tell the king that you'll see him at dinner."

Cinders ticked off the names on her fingers. Yes. It was definitely Andy who was speaking.

"And what will *I* do?" Cinders asked as the sisters began to busy themselves around her rooms.

"Whatever you like!" Andy replied. "You're practically a princess."

"Practically a princess," Cinders repeated.

"With absolutely nothing to do."

She watched as the sisters set to work and wondered, just for a moment, what her own stepsisters might be doing. Who would wash the dishes if she wasn't there to do it? Who would chop the wood and feed the pigs?

With nothing else to do, she sat quietly in a chair and gazed out the window while the sisters got on with their chores. There had to be something beyond the mountains, she thought to herself.

But whatever could it be?

Chapter Fifteen

FROM THE MOMENT SHE set foot out of bed the next morning, Cinders's day went from bad to worse.

First, she tried to take Sparks for a walk and find the spot where her parents had met, but everywhere she tried to go was forbidden.

Then she ran away when the palace photographers tried to take her photograph for the terrible magazines her sisters liked to read.

And then she was told off for running on the palace grounds because "it wasn't considered ladylike."

And, right after that, she was told off for saying something very naughty to the guard who had told her off for running when she thought he couldn't hear her anymore.

"What's the point in having a garden if you can't play in it?" she asked Sparks as she returned to her rooms to stare out the window. "Imagine going to the bother of having an entire garden that's just for looking at. What a lot of nonsense."

"Imagine having an entire kitchen full of food downstairs when I'm starving," he replied, rolling onto his back and letting his floppy red legs fall to the floor. "Wish us up a sausage, Cinders. I won't make it if I don't get something to eat soon."

"I'm hungry too," Cinders said, rubbing her own empty belly, "but I really, really don't think it's a good idea to make wishes while we're in the palace."

It seemed Sparks had changed his mind on that front.

"But I'm starving," he cried, throwing his head back and howling at the ceiling. "My kingdom for a sausage!"

"Shush, Sparks!" Cinders leaped across the room and clamped her hand around his chops. "If the guards hear you, they'll take you away and then you'll be *in* the sausages, not eating them. Now, do you promise to be quiet?"

Sparks nodded and she let go. Immediately, he began to howl.

"I wish we had some sausages!" Cinders shouted.

Her fingertips tickled and, when she looked down at the floor, she saw one measly-looking, skinny sausage.

"That's the best you can do?" Sparks asked, poking at it with a paw. "Good grief."

"You're welcome," she replied as he gobbled it up. Holding her hands up to the light of the window, Cinders sighed.

Why weren't her wishes working any-more?

And where oh where was Brian when she needed her?

Chapter Sixteen

"**I REALLY DO THINK SOMETHING** a bit looser might be more appropriate for dinner," Cinders said as Andy, Mandy, and Sandy helped her downstairs to the dining room. Candy and Tandy were already preparing her chamber for bedtime while Sparks resumed his very important nap. "Not that it isn't a lovely dress, but come on—don't you think it's a bit much?"

The dress was a bit more than a bit much. Canary yellow and with fourteen layers of silk skirts, Cinders felt as though she were drowning in it.

"The queen specifically asked that you wear this dress," Mandy replied, slapping Cinders's hand away from the very, very, very tight corset. "And you look so pretty. I'm sure you'll get used to it very soon."

"If it doesn't squeeze the life out of me first," Cinders muttered. "Death by ball gown. I can see the headlines now."

"Cinderella." The king stood as she entered the room, and she tried very hard to give a small bow without dropping the ridiculous wig Andy had insisted she wear. "Don't you scrub up nicely?"

"I feel a bit . . ." She paused and turned her head to look at the queen.

There she was, sitting at the head of a long, narrow, gilded table, wearing an almost-identical dress and wig.

"I feel beautiful, thank you," Cinders said, smiling so brightly that the king began to wonder if there might be something wrong with her. "This is the most glorious dress I've ever seen, and who knew wigs could be so much fun?"

They weren't fun, not in the slightest. She was hot and sticky and she could barely hold up her own head, but she was also starving and, as every right-minded person knows, food comes first. Cinders was quite prepared to suffer a corset and a sweaty head if it meant filling her belly.

"You look lovely," Joderick whispered from across the table as she trotted down the length of the room. "But the wig's a bit much."

Cinders smiled and took her seat across

from the prince. The king and queen were so far away from them at the other end of the table that she could barely even hear them.

"Have you had a nice day?" she asked, really hoping he had. This wasn't Joderick's fault after all, and she really did want at least one friend in the palace.

"No," he admitted. "I was in a very important meeting all day. It's supposed to be top secret, but since we're to be married, I'm sure I can tell you."

"Ooh!" Cinders was terrible at keeping secrets, but she hated to be left out. "Tell me everything."

"It's the fairies," Joderick whispered. "It turns out they're real and something must be done about them."

"Fairies?" Cinders gulped. "What's wrong with fairies?"

"What's wrong with fairies?" Joderick looked shocked. "They're terrible things. Monsters even! Didn't you know?"

Cinders reached across the table and grabbed a big frosted pastry.

"I did not know that," she said, shoving the pastry in her mouth and trying not to look too scared. "Please tell me more."

"The fairies want to take over our kingdom," the prince explained. "And we have to keep them away before they sneak over the mountains and eat us all up in our beds!"

"Eat us all up?" Cinders gulped. Fairies wanted to *eat* people? Brian was weird, but she'd never given off much of a cannibal vibe.

"Yes," Joderick confirmed. "They have long claws and sharp teeth and they steal naughty children out of their beds at night."

"Oh my," she said. "Is that right?"

"They're terrible things, the fairies," said Joderick, shaking his head sadly. "We've managed to keep them away for generations, but my father is worried they could come back and attack any day. Jack suggested we all go up the beanstalk and live in the sky, but that's hardly practical."

Cinders was still thinking hard. None of this fairy business made sense to her. Brian was a fairy and Brian didn't have claws or sharp teeth, and the only thing she'd tried to eat was a plateful of sausages. Admittedly, she had very questionable fashion sense, but that didn't make her a monster.

"Have you ever *met* a fairy?" she asked Jodders as he loaded his plate with broccoli, peas, and string beans. "Maybe they're not as bad as you think."

"No one has met one, not for more than one hundred years," he replied. "Not since my great-great-grandfather made a pact to

stop them from coming to our land, and I think I'd like to keep it that way, thank you very much."

Cinders didn't know what to say. Could it be true? Could Brian really be so wicked? It seemed rather unlikely. Not lovely Brian. Flaky, yes. Unreliable, absolutely. But a kiddy-eating monster? Not so much.

"What are you two whispering about?" the king called down the long golden table.

"Nothing," Joderick piped up quickly. "We definitely weren't talking about fairies."

"Oh, good," the king replied. "Keep that stuff to yourself, son."

"Thank you for dinner," Cinders said, pointing at all the food on the table. "I say, this is a lovely spread, isn't it?"

"This is nothing," the king said. "Wait until you see the whole suckling pig Cook is preparing."

"Ooh, that sounds nice," she said, rubbing her still-rumbling tummy. Without thinking, she added, "I wish it was ready now."

Quick as a flash, Cook walked in, carrying a whole suckling pig.

"Dinner is served," she declared, looking a bit surprised when met with a round of thunderous applause.

"What a coincidence," Cinders said, covering her sparkling hands with a napkin. Why were her wishes coming true *now*? She shoved another pastry in her mouth. At least if she was eating she couldn't make any more accidental wishes.

"Bravo, Cook," the king said as Cook prepared to carve. "It looks so good I wish it would run down the table and jump right into my mouth!"

Underneath her napkin, Cinders felt the familiar fluttering feeling in her fingers. Golden sparkles flew from her hands all the way down the table and showered the suckling pig. With an indignant *oink!* it opened its eyes, jumped up from the plate, and ran down the table, directly toward the king.

"Somebody stop that pig!" the king wailed, leaping out of his seat and running away. "Stop the pig!"

The queen leaped toward the regicidal hog with a look of determination, only to slip in a puddle of applesauce and fall right back down on her queenly posterior. Cinders stared in horror as the pig bore down on the king and bit him right on the behind.

"I wish the pig would **STOP!**" she

yelled, sending another scattering of sparkles toward her dashing dinner. At once the
pig froze, one leg in midair, just as he was
about to take another big old bite out of the

king's royal bottom.

"*You!*" The king turned to stare at Cinders, two bright red spots appearing on his cheeks. "It was you!"

Chapter Seventeen

"**U**M. NOT REALLY," CINDERS said. "I don't think."

"Yes it was! You cast a spell!" the king insisted. "What are you, a witch?"

"I didn't *cast* a spell," Cinders replied, slowly realizing what had happened. "You made a wish and I granted it. By accident."

"She's a witch!" the king insisted. Joderick looked at his new friend, evidently uncertain of what to say or do. "She's a witch and witches must be locked up! Guards, seize her!"

"But I'm not a witch," Cinders argued as she backed away. "And, quite frankly, I don't think witches are nearly as bad as you think. There's one living in the woods near us and she's ever so nice, always gives me a card on my birthday. Her name's Veronica and she's a delight. Of course there was all that nonsense with Hansel and Gretel, but Hansel was totally in the wrong there: everyone knows he ate her gingerbread door and then made up the thing about the kidnapping and the oven to get out of trouble."

"She'll be defending fairies next," the queen said, grabbing her butter knife and thrusting it forward to defend herself. "Guards, take her away!"

The two guards on either side of the door looked at each other uncertainly, as if they were there for purely decorative purposes and unsure about tackling an unpredictable, if very little, witch.

"Joderick, I promise I'm not a witch,"

Cinders said, eyeing the floating pig in the middle of the room. To be fair, she could understand why they were all a bit confused. "Please don't let them lock me up!"

Just then there was a commotion outside in the hallway. Her trusty best friend bounded into the dining hall, knocking over the guards in their shiny suits of armor as he ran full throttle toward Cinders.

"Never fear! Sparks is here!"

"A talking dog!" the king shrieked. "She's definitely a witch!"

"I think it's time to leave," Sparks said, pausing to nab a string of sausages. "*What?*" he asked as Cinders arched an eyebrow at him, making her way toward the door. "I came to save you, didn't I? No harm in grabbing a snack on the way."

"Guards!" squeaked the king. "GUARDS!"

"Yes, *guards*!" squeaked the queen. "Guards, guards!"

"Oof," groaned one of them. "Can't get up. Give us a hand, Georgie."

"All those pumpkins, Peter." Georgie staggered to his feet and stuck out his hand, puffing as he tried to pull Peter to his feet. "That's what it is, innit? You're a bit squished in that there armor."

"You're a fine one to talk, Georgie!" huffed Peter, struggling to stand up. "*You* ate all the pudding *and* all the pies— Oi!" Peter snatched at Cinders, who was sidling toward the doorway, lost his balance, and pulled Georgie on top of him with a crash.

"Cinders!" yelped Sparks. "Come *on*!"

"Jodders!" yelled Cinders, turning to her new friend. "Are you coming with me?"

"Don't even think about it, son!" yelled the king.

"Yes!" yelled the queen. "Don't you dare leave with that girl!"

Joderick looked from Cinders to his

parents, then back to her. Then he smiled and ran over to Cinders.

"Joderick Jorenson Picklebottom!" shouted the queen. "Don't move another muscle!"

The guards were clanking to their feet, but kept pulling each other over, crashing this way and that, still shouting about too many pumpkins and pecks of pickled peppers.

"Quick!" said Joderick to Cinders, dashing for the door. "Follow me!" He tore out of the dining room and into the hallway, ignoring his shrieking mother and furious father, even though he knew he'd probably be grounded for all time.

"Thanks, Joderick," Cinders said, hurtling after him and tearing off her wig and loosening her corset as she ran.

"Hurry," panted Sparks. "Before those guards are back on their feet."

"This way." Joderick pulled on a candelabra and a small, Sparks-size door opened in the wall underneath it. "This tunnel leads all the way to the stables. No one will know where you've gone."

Sparks leaped into the tunnel without a second thought and disappeared into the darkness.

"My dress is too big!" exclaimed Cinders, trying to wedge herself into the narrow stone doorway. "I'll never fit."

"Here." Joderick pulled off his jacket and his trousers. "Put these on instead."

Cinders looked at the crown prince of the

kingdom, standing before her in his shirt-sleeves and long johns. He had never looked more regal.

"Thank you, Jodders," she said, swapping clothes with her new friend. "Thank you for everything. I want you to know I would never have done anything to hurt you or your family. At least not on purpose. Even if I laughed a little bit when the pig bit your dad's behind."

"He'll survive," Joderick said, almost smiling. "When you get to the stables, grab your horse and head east. Whatever you do, don't go west or you'll end up in the Dark Forest."

"Will I see you again?" Cinders asked, suddenly sad at the thought of leaving her friend behind. "And won't you be in terrible trouble?"

"I have a feeling you will see me again," he replied, turning as the sound of the guards' footsteps thundered up the hallway. "And I have a feeling I *will* be in trouble. Unless I can come up with a story—it wouldn't be the first time. Now *go*, before they catch you!"

Cinders took a deep breath, closed her eyes, and jumped headfirst into the pitch black of the tunnel.

Chapter Eighteen

"**WE'VE SEARCHED THE ENTIRE** kingdom, Your Highness," the head guard announced as he and his army returned to the throne room. "There's no sign of Cinderella, her dog, or her horse."

"Don't stop searching!" the king ordered. "No one goes to sleep until she's been found. I will not have a witch roaming wild in my kingdom."

He'd been pacing up and down ever since Joderick had explained how the girl had put a spell on him to make him help her, and then disappeared into thin air outside the dining hall.

It was witchcraft all right and the king was almost certain that, somehow, those fairies were involved as well.

"We believe she may have gone toward the mountains, Your Highness," the guard went on. "We found tracks that led right up to the edge of the forest."

"The Deep Dark Scary Forest?" the king asked.

The guards nodded.

"At the bottom of the Dark Mountains?" the queen asked.

The guards nodded.

Joderick sighed. Exactly what he'd told Cinders *not* to do.

"Then she's a goner," the queen said, almost happily. "Nothing can survive in those woods, not even a witch."

But Prince Joderick wasn't so sure. If anyone could survive in the Deep Dark Very Incredibly Scary Forest, he was fairly certain it was Cinders.

"Cinderella is officially exiled from this kingdom," the king declared. "Inform her family."

"I'll go," Joderick offered. "I'd like to tell them myself."

The king shrugged. "I was thinking we'd send a text, but all right, if you must."

"We still need him married by midsummer's eve," the queen reminded her husband as Joderick left the throne room. "I'm certain the fairies are behind this plot somehow."

"Me too," the king agreed. "Don't worry, this time we'll take matters into our own hands and find him a far more suitable match."

Chapter Nineteen

"**THIS DOESN'T SEEM LIKE** a very good idea to me," Sparks said as they trotted up to the trees at the edge of the Dark Forest.

"It doesn't seem to me like we have a lot of choice," Cinders said, high atop Mouse the horse. "Unless you want to go back to the palace and live in the dungeons."

"It's you they want to lock up," he reminded her. "Not me."

Mouse squeaked in agreement.

Even though Joderick had said to ride *away* from the mountains, something still drew Cinders in their direction. Before she realized it, they were right at the foothills, surrounded by tall trees that grew up and up and up until

they blocked out any stars in the sky. The air was as cold as ice and the sky was pitch black, and Cinders began to feel a little afraid. But, even so, she knew this was the right direction in which to travel.

"We have to go this way, Sparks," she said very, very quietly as one golden, glittering tear slipped down her cheek. "I can feel it in my bones."

"It's not your bones I'm worried about," he muttered. "It's mine."

"I just wish we could see a bit better," said Cinders. "And had some kind of help."

For the first time, she was beyond thankful when the sparkles shot out from her hands and lit up the forest around her. Or at least she was until she began to float up out of her saddle and hover in mid-air. Sparks covered his eyes with his paws and Mouse ran around and around in circles until he collided with a low tree branch and promptly fell over.

"Oh me, oh my! What's occurring?"

The sparkles subsided and Cinders opened her eyes to see Brian standing in front of her, wearing a neon-pink tracksuit and lime-green rain boots.

"Ah, it's you," the fairy said. "What do you want? I was halfway through mowing my lawn."

"Where have you been?" Cinders gasped. She was relieved to see her fairy godmother, but she was still very upset with her. "I have had the worst day of my entire life."

"Did you not just hear me?" Brian asked. "I said I was mowing my lawn and it's not one of those fancy ride-on mowers, so don't go acting like you're the only one who's had a rough day. What's the matter with you?"

"I went to the ball, I met the prince, then the prince asked me to marry him and I had to go and live at the palace, and then I accidentally wished a roasted pig back to life and it bit the king on the bottom!" Cinders paused to take a deep breath. "He accused me of being a witch, we ran away, and now we're stuck out here, in these woods, with no idea what to do or where to go."

"You did all that in one day?" Brian looked surprised. **"BLIMEY."**

"What are you talking about?" Cinders yelped. "It's been a week!"

"Are you sure?" Brian asked, frowning in concentration. "Definitely doesn't feel as though it's been that long to me. Two days tops. I mean, I have a big garden but still."

"It's been seven very long days," Sparks corrected her, nodding. "Trust me."

"Hmm." Brian raised a glittery eyebrow. "Interesting."

"And now the king wants me locked up!" Cinders threw her tingling fingertips into Brian's face. "And, in case you haven't noticed, I'm currently flying!"

"Of course you're not a witch," Brian scoffed, patting Mouse the horse on the rump and then giving his mane a sniff. "You're a fairy. Now is it me or does this horse smell like cheese?"

Cinders began to float slowly back down to the ground.

"I'm . . . a . . . *what*?" she asked slowly.

"You're a fairy," Brian replied. "Or at least you're a half fairy. Your mother was a fairy and your dad is, well, a bit simple, but nice enough for a human."

"I'm a *fairy*?" Cinders repeated.

"Can you grant wishes?" Brian asked.

Cinders nodded. "Mine *and* other people's, it turns out."

"Do you have a very, very sweet tooth?" Brian asked.

Cinders nodded. "Even now I could murder a chocolate chip cookie."

"And do you own a talking dog?" Brian asked.

"I'll say yes to that one," Sparks replied.

"So if we add in the fact that your mother was a fairy, I think we can conclude that you, Cinderella, are also a fairy," Brian said. "Unfortunately, you also take after your father, so you have a tendency to be a bit dense. I mean, your mom just told him to keep you away from the palace and he never questioned it? Hopeless. But you? I honestly can't believe you haven't worked it out before now."

"This explains everything," Cinders gasped, finally putting two and two together. "And I bet all fairies have really smelly feet, just like me, right?"

"Um, sure, why not?" Brian said, wrinkling her nose.

"They really are disgusting," Sparks commented, holding his nose with his paws. "Always been foul. It's not right for a young girl to have such stinking socks."

"Right . . ." said Brian.

Cinders's head was spinning. She was a fairy. Her mother had been a fairy. It really was quite a lot to take in on an almost-empty stomach.

"Why don't I have wings like you?" she asked.

"What exactly have you done to deserve a pair of wings, young lady?" Brian scolded. "Kids today, expecting everything on a plate as soon as they snap their fingers. . . ."

"Okay, I'll wait on the wings," Cinders

said. "But why does the king think fairies have claws and fangs and that they eat people for dinner? Whatever happened between the Fairy King and King Picklebottom all those years ago?"

Brian rolled her eyes and shook her wings, leaving a circle of glitter all around her.

"Some people never get over a breakup," she said, sighing. "Trust me, it's just bad publicity. We don't have fangs, we don't have claws, and we definitely don't eat humans. Not really much for the savory options at all, to be honest—we're definitely dessert people. As you might have noticed, all fairies have a sweet tooth."

"Jodders told me there've been no fairies in our kingdom for more than a hundred years," Cinders said. She had never been so confused in her life. "So how did my parents find each other at the palace? They did meet at the palace, right . . . ?" It was the only thing her dad had ever told her. If that turned out to be a lie . . .

"Oh, yes, they did," said Brian. "Your mom left Fairyland and came over here. Probably passed this very spot on her way. But it's an awfully long story. Are you sure you want to hear it now?"

"Yes!" Cinders exclaimed. "I want to hear everything! Why did my mother leave Fairyland? How did she come to meet my father? Please tell me everything."

"I would, only I was thinking you might want to get out of the forest before nightfall," Brian suggested. "Because that's when the gadzoozles and nobbledizooks come out to hunt."

"And that's bad, is it?" Cinders asked, looking around nervously.

"Depends," her fairy godmother replied. "Do you like being hung upside down and roasted over an open fire?"

"Not especially," Cinders answered.

"Then I should get a wriggle on," Brian said, looking at her watch. "The journey to Fairyland won't be easy for a halfling, but your magic will get stronger as you get closer to home. And, if you're ever in desperate need of help, you must eat cake. Cake boosts your magic, as you might have worked out by now."

Staring into the darkness of the forest, Cinders felt herself shiver from top to toe.

What she wouldn't have given for one of Joderick's chocolate brownies right at that moment.

"Can't you take me there yourself?" she asked. "I could help you finish mowing that lawn."

"It doesn't work like that, I'm afraid," Brian replied, shaking her head. "And because you're only a half-ling you won't be able to wish yourself in either. You need to quest through the Dark Forest, traverse the Empty Valley, and then travel along the mountain pass if you want to make it to Fairyland."

"Sounds a bit too dangerous to me," Sparks said gruffly. Mouse twitched his whiskers and flicked his tail in agreement. "Perhaps we should pop back to the palace and see if all the fuss has died down?"

"And spend the rest of our lives in the dungeons?" Cinders reminded him. "They wanted to lock me up when they thought I was a witch. Imagine what the king would do if he found out I was a fairy!"

"Maybe the dungeons aren't all that bad," Sparks suggested, cowering at the thought of venturing into the

Dark Forest. "Did you even get a good look at them? If each cell has its own TV, I say we give it a try."

But Cinders had made up her mind. There was no going back—she could only go onward. If her mother had braved these woods and journeyed through the valley and along the mountain pass—even if it had been in the opposite direction—then so would she.

"No, Sparks, it's time to find out who I really am," she told her four-legged friend as she climbed back into Mouse's saddle. "We go on to Fairyland."

"Righto." Brian clapped happily before checking her watch. "Would you look at the time? I must dash, but do shout if you need anything. I probably won't come right away, but I'll give it a shot. And don't worry about the munklepoops—their bark is worse than their bite."

"The munklepoops?" Cinders suddenly felt far less bold than she had just a moment before.

"Yes, big things, lots of teeth, very bad breath," Brian explained, wrinkling her nose again. "Wait, did I get it the wrong way around? Yes I did. Bite is worse than their bark. Awfully quiet things, they are. You hardly know they're there and then snap, there goes your leg. Anyway, I must dash. See you soon."

And

   with

      that

        she

          was

            gone.

Chapter Twenty

"**I**'M STARTING TO WISH we'd never met her. Why is it she never shows up with good news?" Sparks asked, a little shaky on his paws. He nuzzled his head under Cinders's arm and stared up at her with big, shining eyes. "Come on, let's go home."

"If we go back now, we'll never find out the truth about my mother," Cinders explained to her dithering dog, "and I might never learn how to use my powers properly."

"Or safely," Sparks added reluctantly. He looked back toward the kingdom and felt his tail droop. He knew there was no going home again. "I hate to harp on about this, but before we make a final decision, can we get a firm yes or no on whether or not they have sausages in Fairyland? I heard a lot of talk about cake, but there wasn't any solid information on sausages."

"I don't know," Cinders admitted. "But if I'm able to control my magic I'll be able to

get you as many sausages as you like, won't I? Forever."

"You do make an excellent point." His ears perked up for a second until a wild howl echoed through the trees, rustling every leaf on every branch. Mouse the horse spun around, chasing his tail in a very mouse-like way as Sparks shivered from the tip of his nose to the end of his toes.

"I know you're scared," said Cinders to both of them, trying to look as brave as possible, "but as long as we stick together I think we'll be okay."

"I'm not afraid of anything," the dog barked, puffing out his fur to make himself as big as possible. "Munklepoops, gadzoozles, and nobbledizooks? I've seen your stepmother first thing in the morning—it'll take more than a monster from the Dark Forest to scare this doggo."

A sudden shaking of the leaves made everyone jump.

"What was that?"

Sparks leaped high into the air and dashed behind Cinders.

"I thought you weren't afraid of anything?" she asked the petrified pup before reaching down to yank off one of her shoes. She brandished it high above her head, ready to strike. There was definitely someone or something hiding in the bushes.

"I'm protecting you," Sparks explained with chattering teeth. "In case they sneak up from behind. What are you doing with your shoe?"

"I'm going to use it as a weapon," Cinders

whispered, batting the shoe up and down like a hammer. "You know, like this."

"You're more likely to knock them out with the stench," he muttered, covering his nose with one large red paw.

Another rustle and Sparks cowered behind his best friend. There was nowhere to run and nowhere to hide. All they could do was face the thing.

"Hello? Who's there?" Cinders called, full of hope that whatever was about to show itself would be friendly. What if it was Joderick, come to help? Or her father! Or, good golly gosh, she'd even prefer the sight of her step-mother to a munklepoop.

Very, very, very slowly, a red-faced boy in a familiar hat rose up from behind a bush.

"Hello," he said. "Cinders, what on earth are you doing with your shoe?"

"Hansel!" she yelled. "You scared the living daylights out of us!"

"Not me," panted Sparks, flopping to the ground in a trembling heap.

Hansel tumbled out of the bushes, brushing stray leaves and twigs out of his green felt hat, which, quite frankly, Cinders had always thought looked a bit silly. He puffed up his chest and planted his hands on his hips.

"Cinders!" he bellowed. "It is I, Hansel, and I am here to save you."

"Save me from what?" she asked, jamming her foot back into her shoe.

"Um," he glanced around, looking for an immediate threat. "I'm not really sure."

"Right," Cinders replied with a sigh. "So what are you really doing all the way out here? Did you eat part of the witch's cottage again?"

Hansel looked outraged. "No, of course not!"

Cinders raised an eyebrow in disbelief. She knew a lie when she heard one.

"I don't have time for this!" Hansel threw a panicked look over his shoulder. "And I did not eat any part of the witch's cottage. Anyone could have popped one of those roof tiles off for a tasty snack. And, really, what kind of monster makes a cottage out of gingerbread and expects people *not* to eat it?"

"Right, so you did eat part of Veronica's cottage," Cinders said, her arms folded in front of her. This was just what she didn't need. Hansel had always been a pain, ever since they were little. She hadn't forgiven him for the time he'd set off that magic porridge pot. The entire village had had to eat porridge for days, and she still couldn't bear to look at a bowl of it.

"Okay, look," he said. "*Someone* who is not me *may* have eaten a *tiny* bit of the witch's roof, and a pigeon *may* have gotten in and pooped on her head when she was asleep. So the long and the short of it is I need to get gone."

"Oh, he really is the worst," Sparks grumbled. "Why is there never a hungry nobbledizook around when you need one?"

Hansel stared at Sparks. "Cinders," he said shakily, "did you know your dog could talk?"

"Yeah, I know. The thing is, it's all a bit complicat—"

"You know what?" said Hansel. "I'm in a hurry, so I'm just going to roll with it. You can explain everything later." He turned to look at Mouse the horse. "Can you guys give me a ride?"

"Just *so* rude," huffed Sparks.

From somewhere outside the forest, Cinders heard the echo of loud and angry voices.

"I'm on the run too," she said, clambering

up into the saddle on Mouse's back. "You'd just get in the way."

"Not necessarily. Maybe I can help. Where are you going? You look like you're off on a quest. Are you going on a quest? Do you need a brave leader who can find the way to anywhere?" Hansel batted his very long eyelashes. "If so, I'm your man."

Cinders snorted. "The only thing you're good for is telling fibs and getting on the wrong side of witches. Anyway, I'm going to Fairyland and you can't possibly help with that."

"Not true!" Hansel yelled. "I've been to Fairyland loads of times."

"Lie number one," Sparks said politely.

"Well, how about this?" Hansel fumbled

with the clasp on his knapsack. "I've got travel snacks! I'm totally useful! You could not do without me!" He opened the leather satchel and showed Cinders what was inside. It was cake. Glorious, glorious cake. And a very suspicious-looking slab of gingerbread.

"Well, that does change things," she admitted. Whether he'd nicked it from Veronica the witch or not, it did look delicious.

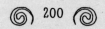

"Hmm," said Sparks. "It's not as good as a sausage, is it?"

Hansel smiled and lifted up his ill-gotten gingerbread. Under it were loads of little sausages. "I never go anywhere without a dozen sausages," he said.

"I've changed my mind—he's in," declared Sparks.

"The tracks lead this way!"

The voices beyond the tree line were getting louder. Whoever it was would find them any second.

Cinders looked at Hansel. Hansel looked at Cinders.

"Come on," Sparks barked, nodding toward the dark of the forest. "If we're going, let's go. Last one to Fairyland is a rotten munklepoop."

"Please," Hansel pleaded, suddenly looking very serious, "I know you've got no reason to trust me, but I *really* need your help."

"*Fine*," decided Cinders, "but I'm in charge and you are definitely just the side-kick." Taking a deep breath, she held out her

hand and pulled Hansel up onto the back of the horse, where he clung on behind her.

"Straight ahead and quickly," said Hansel before hastily adding, "would be my humble suggestion."

"Straight ahead it is," Cinders agreed, giving

Mouse an encouraging squeeze. They galloped off, with Sparks dashing through the trees beside them, leaving their pursuers far behind.

Even though she had no idea what lay ahead, Cinders felt a determined smile spreading across her face. As long as she kept believing in herself and had Sparks by her side, there was nothing she couldn't do. She was half fairy, after all.

And, while she didn't know how long it would take to find Fairyland or what might happen on the way there, Cinders knew one thing: this time she was setting off on a *real* ADVENTURE. . . .

TURN THE PAGE FOR A SNEAK PEEK AT THE NEXT BOOK IN THE SERIES!

Chapter One

"HANSEL!" CINDERS SQUEALED. "IF you don't loosen your grip, you're going to be walking the rest of the way to Fairyland."

"Perhaps you ought to let me be in front for a while," Hansel replied, slackening his arms just a little. "I'm very strong and I wouldn't mind if you needed to hold on to me to feel safe."

"You're going to need more than something to hold on to to feel safe in a minute,"

Cinders muttered back. "My horse, my quest, my rules."

Cinders was on a very important mission to find out some *very* important things, and it was bad enough having to listen to Sparks, her magical talking dog, rattle on about sausages, or lack thereof, without a boy in a silly hat giving her grief. Every time Mouse the horse (Mouse was a mouse who Cinders had accidentally turned into a horse, but that was another story altogether) took a sharp turn to avoid running into a tree or off the edge of a cliff, Hansel would let out a terrible shriek and squeeze Cinders's waist so tight she thought she might snap in two.

"Perhaps you shouldn't have invited him along in the first place," Sparks suggested from

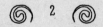

his comfortable position curled up in front of Cinders, his muzzle resting in Mouse's mane.

"Excuse me, you were the one who said he should come along when he offered you those sausages," Cinders reminded him. "Honestly, Sparks, I don't think there's anything you wouldn't do for a sausage."

Sparks considered this for a moment, decided there was a good chance that she might be right, and so said nothing.

It felt as though they'd been riding for days, but really it had only been a few hours since Cinders had escaped King Picklebottom's guards and fled the palace. But, as they rode deeper into the forest and the air grew chilly, she was starting to wonder if they'd made the right decision. Long, spindly branches wove themselves together overhead, blocking out the sun, and the farther they went, the darker and darker and darker the sky became until Cinders could barely see her hand in front of her face.

Thankfully, she was very, very brave. Most of the time. She wasn't afraid of anything — King Picklebottom, the Dark Forest, munklepoops, gadzoozles, or nobbledizooks. Not that she'd ever been in the Dark Forest before or met a munkle-poop, gadzoozle, or nobbledizook in real life. All she knew was that she had to get to Fairyland. Just a week ago, she'd been living in the countryside with her father and her stepsisters and her really rather awful step-mother. An ordinary girl with an ordinary life. And then one day, out of nowhere, her fairy godmother had arrived and Cinders had started to develop magic powers, and everything had changed.

"Cinders." Hansel ducked his head to avoid getting slapped in the chops by a low-hanging branch. "Can I ask you a question?"

"Yes, Hansel."

"You said your mom was a fairy?"

"Yes, Hansel."

"Which means you're half fairy?"

"Yes, Hansel."

"So why don't you cast a spell and magic us all to Fairyland rather than ride through the Dark Forest?"

Cinders sighed. If they'd been through this once, they'd been through it a thousand times.

"Because my magic isn't strong enough," she said as she flicked Mouse's reins, encouraging him to go just a little bit faster. "I only found out I was half fairy a week ago. These things don't work themselves out overnight, you know. I mean, if I'd been more in control of my powers, I wouldn't have made that pig come back to life at dinner, I wouldn't have scared the king, he wouldn't have decided I was a witch, and we wouldn't have had to run away in the first place."

Cinders couldn't help but wonder if it wouldn't have been easier to just stay at the palace, marry Prince Joderick, and behave herself. Except she didn't want to marry Prince Joderick, and she never had been very good at behaving herself. But now she was lost in the forest with the palace guards after her, and the only thing she could think to do was go to Fairyland, where her mother apparently came from, and try to get some answers.

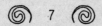 7

"Fair enough, fair enough," said Hansel. He closed his eyes as Mouse leaped over a fallen tree trunk and thundered on, deeper into the forest.

"One more question. Do you think your magic might be strong enough to find us a toilet? I really have to go."